RIVER DAY

by Jane B. Mason
illustrated by Henri Sorensen

Macmillan Publishing Company   New York
Maxwell Macmillan Canada   Toronto
Maxwell Macmillan International   New York   Oxford   Singapore   Sydney

For my mother, who brought me to the Brule
—J.B.M.

For Mie and Cuno
—H.S.

Library of Congress Cataloging-in-Publication Data. Mason, Jane B. River day / by Jane B. Mason ; illustrated by Henri Sorensen. — 1st ed. p. cm. Summary: Alex goes canoeing on the river with her grandfather, in the hope of seeing the bald eagle that is nesting nearby. ISBN 0-02-762869-8 [1. Canoes and canoeing—Fiction. 2. Grandfathers—Fiction. 3. Bald eagle—Fiction. 4. Eagles—Fiction.] I. Sorensen, Henri, ill. II. Title. PZ7.M412Ri 1994 [E]—dc20 93-26573

It was a hot summer day. Alex woke up early, peeked out her bedroom window to check the sky, and smiled. Then she pulled on shorts and a T-shirt and stumbled to the kitchen.

At breakfast, Eli spilled his cereal all over the table.

"Can I go, too?" he asked for the hundred-and-tenth time. Alex was afraid that her mother would give in and say yes. Eli almost always got his way. But not today.

"No, sweetie," she said. "You're going to stay home with me."

After breakfast, Alex sat on the porch with her paddle, waiting.

When Grampa finally came, he was driving his old blue station wagon with a trailer hitched to the back. The green canoe that said MAD RIVER was strapped on tight.

Grampa was grinning from ear to ear when he stepped out of the car. "Blue sky," he said as he scooped Alex into his wrinkled, freckly arms. "Blue enough to swim in, just like I said."

"It's blue, all right." Alex giggled, squeezing Grampa back.

After the gear was piled into the car, they headed down the dirt road and onto the curvy paved one that ran between the rows of tall pine trees. Alex stared out the window as they drove along. "We'll see that eagle this time, Grampa," she said. "I just know it."

"I hope so, Lexie," he answered. "But we can't be sure."

They turned down the bumpy, skinny road that led to the river. "Oh, I'm sure," she said in a serious voice. "Today is the day."

After Grampa had carried the canoe to the river and laid it gently down on the water, Alex climbed into her seat in the bow.

"You're the scout," Grampa said. "Watch for rocks and logs. We don't want to get caught up on anything."

They paddled through a small lake, and Alex stared hard
at the smooth, moving water. It looked like brown sea glass.
The current was slow and the water was shallow. Grampa
pushed the canoe along to keep it from getting stuck on the
sandy bottom.

The current picked up, and Alex had to hang on tight to her paddle so it wouldn't get swept away.

"Rock on our right," Alex called out. It was a large, flat one hiding just below the surface. Streaks of silver and green from the bottoms of other canoes marked the top.

"Good eyes, Lexie," Grampa said as he held his paddle in the water, making the canoe run alongside of it. "I would have missed that rock for sure. It's flat as a pancake *and* it's hiding."

Around a bend, the river was dark and deep. Alex looked over the side, and where her shadow marked the top of the water, she could see straight to the bottom. She watched it change from sand and pebbles to stringy green weeds.

"Witches' hair." Grampa lifted some of the plant out of the water with his paddle.

"I know." Alex rolled her eyes. "Eli likes to wear it on his head."

"That Eli," Grampa said.

"He's a pest," announced Alex.

Suddenly there was a silver flash. "Fish!" she cried. Soon
a hundred flashes darted under the boat and among the
rocks.
Grampa stopped paddling and leaned over the edge.

"Rainbow trout," he said. "See the yellow and pink on the sides?"

Alex squinted hard and almost saw the colors.

"Hmmmm," she answered.

When Alex looked up, the river had widened and tall pines lined the banks. She searched for the giant, bowl-shaped nest. "There it is," she finally whispered, pointing to the top of a tall tree. Nestled in a curved branch was a giant eagle's nest. But Alex couldn't find the telltale white head. "No eagle," she said aloud. "Where do you think she is?"

"Not sure," Grampa answered. "Let's have lunch and wait awhile."

Grampa steered the canoe toward a grassy riverbank, and Alex pulled the lunch basket onto the grass.

"Liverwurst for you," she said, wrinkling her nose. "I don't know how you and Eli can eat that stuff."

"We know a good thing when we taste it." Grampa grinned.

"Well, I'm having peanut butter and cream cheese."

They sat side by side, munching their sandwiches. Alex dangled her bare feet in the cold water while she searched the sky. Grampa's feet rested in the canoe so it wouldn't float away.

"We should get back on the river," Grampa said after a while. "We have a good paddle in front of us."

A large bird caught Alex's eye, and her heart skipped a beat. "Grampa," she said excitedly. But then she saw that it was just a crow.

"I almost forgot," Grampa said suddenly, jumping up to tie the canoe to a nearby tree. "I haven't gone wading. You can't have a river-picnic without wading." He rolled up his pants and put his toes in the water. "Cold!" he shrieked as he made his way to the middle of the river.

"Wait for me," Alex called. She waded out to him, sand squishing between her toes.

A fish nibbled on Alex's ankle, and she tugged on
Grampa's arm. "Look," she whispered.

Grampa peered at the water.

"This is Eli's favorite thing," Alex said. "Except he always
yells and scares them away."

Grampa nodded. "Fish don't like noise."

"Do you think eagles like noise?" Alex asked.

"I'm not sure about that," he answered.

Alex looked at the empty nest, and all at once, her bottom
lip began to tremble.

Grampa leaned over and gave her a shoulder-squeeze.
"We'll come another day," he said. "I promise."

They waded back to shore, and Alex climbed into her seat.

As the canoe drifted slowly downriver, Alex searched the sky and trees. When she turned to look back, the nest was almost invisible among the branches. She picked up her

paddle and dipped it in the river. Droplets fell and decorated the surface with circles. They grew and grew until the edges disappeared.

"Alex," Grampa suddenly whispered in his excited voice. Alex looked up and caught her breath. High in a tree sat a beautiful black bird with a glimmering white head. Tingles ran all the way up Alex's spine as she watched the bird spring from the branch and open her great wings. After a few smooth strokes, the eagle dove straight toward the water. With claws outstretched, she landed feetfirst only a few yards away from the canoe. A moment later, she lifted a flopping fish from the water with a splash.

For just a few seconds, everything stood completely still.
Then the eagle was carrying her catch upriver and
disappearing around a bend. Alex turned to Grampa, whose
eyes were twinkling like crazy.

"When we come again another day," she said, "let's bring
Eli, too."

Grampa nodded, smiling.

Then the two set off downriver, paddling home.